The Best
Train Set Ever

by PAT HUTCHINS

Greenwillow
Read-alone

GREENWILLOW BOOKS
A Division of William Morrow & Company, Inc.
New York

Copyright © 1978 by Pat Hutchins
All rights reserved. No part of this book may be
reproduced or utilized in any form or by any means,
electronic or mechanical, including photocopying,
recording or by any information storage and
retrieval system, without permission in writing from
the Publisher. Inquiries should be addressed to
Greenwillow Books, 105 Madison Ave.,
New York, N.Y. 10016.
Printed in the United States of America

10 9 8 7 6 5 4 3 2 1

Library of Congress Cataloging
in Publication Data

Hutchins, Pat (date)
The best train set ever.

(Greenwillow read-alone books)
Summary: Three stories about a
little boy's birthday, a Halloween
party, and a Fourth of July Christmas party.
[1. Birthdays—Fiction.   2. Halloween—Fiction.
3. Parties—Fiction.   4. Short stories]
I. Title.   PZ7.H96165Be   [E]
76-30672   ISBN 0-688-80086-6
ISBN 0-688-84086-8 lib. bdg.

for SHAUN

Contents

The Train Set

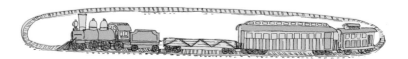

There was a train set
in the window of Mindy's Store.
Every morning
on his way to school
Peter stopped to admire it.

"That sure is the finest train set
I've ever seen," he would say.
"Just look at that engine,
that coach, that flat truck,
that caboose, and that track.
A fine train set like that
must cost a lot of money."

"Come on,"

said his brothers and sisters.

"We'll be late for school."

"What are you getting Peter
 for his birthday?"
 the children asked Ma and Pa.
"He sure wants that train set
 in Mindy's window!"
"We're not telling," said Ma.
"No one can keep a secret
 in this family."

"We've got ten dollars
to spend," said Pa.
"Let's go and see what
the train costs."

"How much is that train set
in the window?" Ma asked.
"Thirty dollars," said Mr. Mindy.
"Too bad." Ma sighed.
"We were hoping
it would be closer to ten."

"The engine costs ten dollars,"
said Mr. Mindy.
"It's a grand engine!"
"It sure is," Pa agreed,
"but not much use on its own."
Ma picked up the engine.
"Well," she said,
"it would be a start."

"What are you getting Peter
for his birthday?"
Anna asked Tony.
"He sure wants that train set."
"I'm not telling," said Tony.
"No one can keep a secret
in this family."

I've saved eight dollars
from helping at the drugstore,
thought Tony. I'll go and see
what the train set costs.

"How much is the train set
in the window?" Tony asked.

"Thirty dollars for the set,"
said Mr. Mindy,

"but we just sold the engine."

"Oh!" said Tony. "I was hoping
it might be around eight."

"The track costs eight dollars,"
  said Mr. Mindy.
"It's the best sort of track."
"It certainly is the best sort
  of track," Tony agreed,
"but not much use on its own."
"It's a start," said Mr. Mindy.

"What are you giving Peter
for his birthday?"
Frank asked Anna.
"He's crazy for that train set."

"I'm not telling," said Anna.
"No one can keep a secret
in this family."

I've saved five dollars
from running errands,
thought Anna.
I'll go and see what it costs.

"How much is that train set
  in the window?" Anna asked.
"Thirty dollars for the set,"
  said Mr. Mindy,
"but I've just sold the engine
  and the track."

"I've only got five dollars," said Anna.

"The coach is five," said Mr. Mindy.

"It's a beautiful coach."

"It's a beautiful coach all right,"
Anna agreed.

"And I guess it's a start!"

"What are you giving Peter
  for his birthday?"
  Maria asked Frank.
"He's mad for that train
  in Mindy's."
"I'm not telling," said Frank.
"No one can keep a secret
  in this family."

I've got four dollars saved,

thought Frank.

I'll go and see what it costs.

"What happened to that train
in the window?" Frank asked.
"I've got four dollars
and I wanted to buy it."

"I've just sold the engine,

the track and the coach,"

said Mr. Mindy,

"but the caboose is four dollars."

"It's a very fine caboose," said Frank,

"but not much use on its own."

"It's a start," said Mr. Mindy.

Maria had three dollars saved.

I'll go and see what

that train set costs, she thought.

"How much is that train set

you had in the window?"

she asked.

"Thirty dollars for the set,"

said Mr. Mindy,

"but I've just sold the engine,

the track, the coach,

and the caboose.

The flat car is all that is left.

But that is three dollars."

"Well," said Maria,

"a flat car's not much use

on its own, but I'll take it."

The next day Peter woke up very early.

Everyone else was still asleep.

I'll just go and look at the train set

he thought, before everyone gets up.

But when he got there the train had gone.

"Too bad." Peter sighed,

and walked slowly home.

"What's wrong?" asked Ma
as he opened the door.
"It's your birthday and you look
as if you've found a nickel
and lost a quarter."

"I've just been to Mindy's,"
said Peter,

"and the train set's gone."

"Is it?" said Ma and Pa.

"Well, here's the engine.
Happy birthday!"

"Gosh!" said Tony.

"I've bought you the track!"

"And I bought you the coach!"
cried Anna.

"I bought you the caboose!"
shouted Frank.

"How about that!" screamed Maria.

"I bought you the flat truck!"

"I told you!" said Ma,

as Peter stared at the parcels.

"No one can keep a secret

in this family.

He hasn't even opened them yet!"

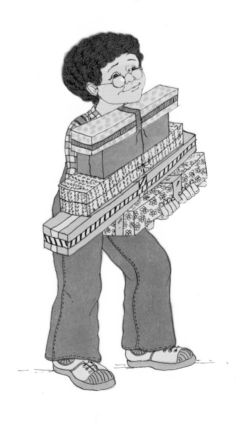

But he soon did, and it certainly was
the finest train set he'd ever seen.

The Halloween Party

"What are you kids
going to wear
to the Halloween party?"
Ma and Pa asked.

"I'm going as a deep-sea diver,"
said Tony.

"I'm going as a hula girl," said Anna.

"I'm going as a wizard," said Frank.

"I'm going as an Indian Chief,"
said Peter.

"I don't know,"
said Maria.

"I'm thinking."

"How do you like my costume?"
said Tony. "I was going to be
a deep-sea diver,
but the flippers are too small.
So I'm going as a spaceman instead."
"It's good," said Maria.
"I wish I could think of something
as good as that."

"Here," said Tony.

"Take the flippers.

   They'll fit you.

   Then you can go

   as a deep-sea diver."

"Thanks," said Maria.

"I'll think about it."

"How do I look?" said Anna.

"Pretty," said Maria. "I wish I could
think of something as pretty as that."

"Here," said Anna. "Take the rest
of the straw. Then you can go
as a hula girl, too."

"Thanks," said Maria.

"I'll think about it."

"Do I make a scary wizard?" said Frank.

"Very," said Maria. "I wish I could
   think of something as scary as that."

"Have this hat," said Frank.

"I made it too small.

   Then you can go as a wizard, too."

"Thanks," said Maria.

"I'll think about it."

"Hi," said Peter. "Do I make
a fine Indian Chief?"
"Very fine," said Maria.
"I wish I could think of
something as fine as that."

"Take the rest of the feathers,"
said Peter. "Then you can go
as an Indian Chief too."
"Thanks," said Maria.
"I'll think about it."

"Where's Maria?" asked Ma and Pa.

"It's time you were going."

"Here I am," said Maria.

"That's good," said Tony.

"And pretty," said Anna.

"And scary," said Frank.

"And fine," said Peter.

"It's the best ostrich
  we've ever seen,"
  said Ma and Pa.

"That ostrich will surely
  win first prize!"
And it did.

A Picnic for Christmas

"Listen to this, kids," said Pa.
"Uncle Joe and Aunt Tina
are going to be in town
for Christmas."

"We'll have a party for them,"
  said Ma, "and have Grandma
  and Grandpa over!"
"And Uncle Matt and Aunt Rosie,"
  said Tony.
"And Cousin Bella
  and Cousin Johnny," said Anna.
"And Greataunt Lil
  and Greatuncle Mike," said Frank.
"And Cousin Billy and Cousin Ida,"
  said Peter.

"How long till they come?"
asked Maria.

"Four days," said Ma.

"I'll go and buy the Christmas tree,"
said Pa.

"I'll ice the cake," said Ma.

"And we'll make the decorations,"

said the children.

"How long till they come?"
  asked Maria.
"Three days," said Ma.
"We'll wrap the presents,"
  said Ma and Pa.
"We'll put up the decorations,"
  said the children.

"How long till they come?"

asked Maria.

"Two days," said Ma.

"Well," said Ma,

"everything is ready

for tomorrow."

"I feel funny," said Peter.

"So do I," said Tony.

"And me," said Anna.

"Me, too," said Frank.

"I don't feel very well either,"

said Maria.

"It's measles," said the doctor.
"Keep them away
from other people
for ten days."

"What about our Christmas party,"
  said the children,
"and Uncle Joe and Aunt Tina?"
"Never mind," said Ma.
"They'll be over again
  in the summer!"
"Summer will never come,"
  said the children.

But it did come.

And they had the best

Fourth of July Christmas Party ever.